Coffee Lovers
STICKERS

Teresa Goodridge

Coffee Lovers
STICKERS

Teresa Goodridge

Dover Publications
Garden City, New York

In this cute little book you'll find 24 sticker pictures of irresistible coffee drinks and treats—a coffee lover's dream! From cappuccino, mocha, and ice cream to the beloved cup of joe, these caffeinated confections will make it clear that coffee is one of life's pleasures. Witty sayings add to the charm. Use the sticker images to add fun touches to notebooks, journals, scrapbook pages, art projects, and much more.

Bibliographical Note
Coffee Lovers Stickers is a new work, first published
by Dover Publications in 2021.

International Standard Book Number
ISBN-13: 978-0-486-84912-6
ISBN-10: 0-486-84912-0

Manufactured in the United States by Phoenix Color
84912001   2021
www.doverpublications.com

Caffeine & Kindness

Fun and Educational Books for the Whole Family!

Coloring & Activity Books

Coloring for All Ages & Interests —
Kids to Adults. Puzzles, Mazes, Dot-to-Dots,
Word Play, Spot-the-Differences,
Hidden Pictures, and More!

Arts, Crafts & Hobbies

Papercrafts, Origami, Drawing, Models,
Science Experiments, Music, and More!

Classic Children's Literature

Fairy Tales, Fables, Stories, Rhymes,
and Riddles!

Browse our titles, download FREE sample pages
and activities, or enter a Dover coloring contest.

www.doverpublications.com

*Celebrating over 75 Years of
Extraordinary Books at Extraordinary Value*

Add some fun to your coffee break!

These cute stickers celebrate the world's most popular beverage! The 24 delightful designs include cappuccino and other classic café drinks, ice cream treats, amusing coffee-related phrases, a colorful collection of coffee cups and mugs, and much more! Espresso enthusiasts and latte lovers alike will find these stickers as enjoyable as their morning cup of joe.

Acid-free inks, paper and adhesives

www.doverpublications.com

$1.99 USA   PRINTED IN THE USA

ISBN-13: 978-0-486-84912-6
ISBN-10: 0-486-84912-0

9 780486 849126

5 0199

CRAFTS & HOBBIES/DECORATING

UPC

8 00759 84912 3